Be with
a book
for a day.

Merely Players

Merely Players

an Anthology of Life Poems
selected by

Lee Bennett Hopkins

ELSEVIER/NELSON BOOKS
New York

Library of Congress Cataloging in Publication Data
Main entry under title:

Merely players.

   1. American poetry. 2. English poetry. 3. Age groups—Poetry. I. Hopkins, Lee Bennett.
PS595.A33M47 1979 821'.008'0354   79-12474
ISBN 0-525-66645-1

Published in the United States by Elsevier/Nelson Books, a division of Elsevier-Dutton Publishing Company, Inc., New York. Published simultaneously in Don Mills, Ontario, by Thomas Nelson and Sons (Canada) Limited.

Printed in the U.S.A.   First Edition
10 9 8 7 6 5 4 3 2 1

ACKNOWLEDGMENTS

Every effort has been made to trace the ownership of all copyrighted material and to secure the necessary permissions to reprint these selections. In the event of any question arising as to the use of any material, the editor and the publisher, while expressing regret for any inadvertent error, will be happy to make the necessary correction in future printings.

Thanks are due to the following for permission to reprint the copyrighted material listed below:

Atheneum Publishers, Inc. for "Shadows" by Patricia Hubbell from *Catch Me a Wind*. Copyright © 1968 by Patricia Hubbell.

Thomas Y. Crowell for "No One Would Believe" by Charlotte Zolotow from *River Winding* by Charlotte Zolotow. Text copyright © 1970 by Charlotte Zolotow.

Curtis Brown, Ltd., for "Boy on a Bus" and "Eighty-Eight" by Lee Bennett Hopkins. Copyright © 1979 by Lee Bennett Hopkins.

Faber and Faber, Limited, for extracts from "Prayer Before Birth" from *The Collected Poems of Louis MacNeice*.

Harcourt Brace Jovanovich, Inc., for "Circles" by Carl Sandburg from *The People, Yes* by Carl Sandburg, copyright 1936 by Harcourt Brace Jovanovich, Inc.; renewed © 1964 by Carl Sandburg; "Gone" by Carl Sandburg from *Chicago Poems* by Carl Sandburg, copyright 1916 by Holt, Rinehart and Winston, Inc.; copyright 1944 by Carl Sandburg.

CONTENTS

INTRODUCTION

At the age of thirty-five, between 1599 and 1600, William Shakespeare created *As You Like It*, one of his most exquisite comedies, containing some of his loveliest poetry.

In Act II, Scene 7, set in the Forest of Arden, Jacques, a courtier attending to the exiled Duke, gives the famous "Seven Ages of Man" monologue; these twenty-eight lines, sharp in imagery, liken the entire existence of human beings to the theater:

> All the world's a stage,
> And all the men and women merely players;
> They have their exits and their entrances;
> And one man in his time plays many parts,
> His acts being seven ages. At first the infant,
> Mewling and puking in the nurse's arms;
> Then the whining school-boy, with his satchel
> And shining morning face, creeping like snail
> Unwillingly to school. And then the lover,
> Sighing like furnace, with a woeful ballad
> Made to his mistress' eyebrow. Then a soldier,
> Full of strange oaths, and bearded like the pard,
> Jealous in houour, sudden and quick in quarrel,

Seeking the bubble reputation
Even in the cannon's mouth. And then the justice,
In fair round belly with good capon lin'd,
With eyes severe and beard of formal cut,
Full of wise saws and modern instances;
And so he plays his part. The sixth age shifts
Into the lean and slipper'd pantaloon,
With spectacles on nose and pouch on side;
His youthful hose, well sav'd, a world too wide
For his shrunk shank; and his big manly voice,
Turning again toward childish treble, pipes
And whistles in his sound. Last scene of all,
That ends this strange eventful history,
Is second childishness and mere oblivion;
Sans teeth, sans eyes, sans taste, sans everything.

Certainly these perceptive words can be viewed as an analogy, as fresh and meaningful today as they were almost four hundred years ago.

Merely Players reflects these seven ages: Birth, Childhood, Love, War, Adulthood, Aged, and Death. Within this anthology, over three centuries of poets and their work are represented—poetry as diverse as the stages and ages we live and pass through.

From "Birth/At first..." through "Death/Last scene of all..." encompasses and reveals life-styles and patterns known to all of us, images we might never have thought about or seen before, common things—of people and of thoughts.

Works by American and European voices are heard, including timeless classics by such well-known eighteenth- and nineteenth-century masters as William Blake, Robert and Elizabeth Barrett Browning, Percy Bysshe Shelley. Also represented are twentieth-century American Pulitzer-Prize-winning poets—Gwendolyn Brooks, Carl Sandburg, Louis Simpson, William Carlos Williams, and Gary Snyder. Contemporary voices of Langston Hughes, Patricia Hubbell, and Nikki Giovanni are among those heard.

All the world *is* a stage—a stage on which life moves by far too quickly. We, as merely players, must take our time for and with each age—exploring, searching, reaching, sharing our newly discovered visions with others as poets aptly do.

No matter who we are, we are players, but there are parts we can portray only through the poets' pens.

Lee Bennett Hopkins

ONE

BIRTH

"At first. . ."

All the world's a stage,
And all the men and women merely players;
They have their exits and their entrances;
And one man in his time plays many parts,
His acts being seven ages. At first the infant,
Mewling and puking in the nurse's arms;

William Shakespeare

from
PRAYER BEFORE BIRTH

I am not yet born; provide me
With water to dandle me, grass to grow for me,
   trees to talk to me, sky to sing to me, birds and
      a white light in the back of my mind to guide me.

*   *   *   *

I am not yet born; rehearse me
In the parts I must play and the cues I must take when
   old men lecture me, bureaucrats hector me,
         mountains frown at me, lovers laugh at me,
            the white waves call me to folly
               and the desert calls me to doom
                  and the beggar refuses my gift
                     and my children curse me.

Louis MacNeice

MANHATTAN LULLABY
(for Richard—one day old)

Now lighted windows climb the dark,
    The streets are dim with snow,
Like tireless beetles, amber-eyed,
    The creeping taxis go.
Cars roar through caverns made of steel,
    Shrill sounds the siren horn,
And people dance and die and wed—
    and boys like you are born.

Rachel Field

from
HAMLET

We know what we are,
  but know not what we may be.

William Shakespeare

TWO

CHILDHOOD

" . . . shining morning face. . ."

Then the whining school-boy, with his satchel
And shining morning face, creeping like snail
Unwillingly to school.

William Shakespeare

SHADOWS

Chunks of night
Melt
In the morning sun.
One lonely one
Grows legs
And follows me
To school.

Patricia Hubbell

from
CITY TALK

These are
Two happy times—
Watching a baseball game,
Seeing your baby brother walking
Alone.

John Vitale

THE FIRST DAY OF SCHOOL

"Write a composition,"
said the teacher,
"about something you did
during summer vacation.
Make it two pages long
and neatness counts."

I sat there
remembering the quiet
of the giant redwoods.
Even my little brother
whispered.

"Teacher,
could I write a poem
instead?"

Bobbi Katz

KNOXVILLE, TENNESSEE

I always like summer
best
you can eat fresh corn
from daddy's garden
and okra
and greens
and cabbage
and lots of
barbecue
and buttermilk
and homemade ice-cream
at the church picnic
and listen to
gospel music
outside
at the church
homecoming
and go to the mountains with
your grandmother
and go barefooted
and be warm
all the time
not only when you go to bed
and sleep

Nikki Giovanni

THIS IS JUST TO SAY

I have eaten
the plums
that were in
the icebox

and which
you were probably
saving
for breakfast

Forgive me
they were delicious
so sweet
and so cold

William Carlos Williams

KANSAS BOY

This Kansas boy who never saw the sea
Walks through the young corn rippling at his knee
As sailors walk; and when the grain grows higher
Watches the dark waves leap with greener fire
Than ever oceans hold. He follows ships,
Tasting the bitter spray upon his lips,
For in his blood up-stirs the salty ghost
Of one who sailed a storm-bound English coast.
Across wide fields he hears the sea winds crying,
Shouts at the crows—and dreams of white gulls
   flying.

Ruth Lechlitner

PETE AT THE ZOO

I wonder if the elephant
Is lonely in his stall
When all the boys and girls are gone
And there's no shout at all,
And there's no one to stamp before,
No one to note his might.
Does he hunch up, as I do,
Against the dark of night?

Gwendolyn Brooks

YOUNG NIGHT THOUGHT

All night long and every night,
When my mamma puts out the light,
I see the people marching by,
As plain as day, before my eye.

Armies and emperors and kings,
All carrying different kinds of things,
And marching in so grand a way,
You never saw the like by day.

So fine a show was never seen,
At the great circus on the green;
For every kind of beast and man
Is marching in that caravan.

At first they move a little slow,
But still the faster on they go,
And still beside them close I keep
Until we reach the town of Sleep.

Robert Louis Stevenson

THREE

LOVE

"And then the lover. . ."

And then the lover,
Sighing like furnace, with a woeful ballad
Made to his mistress' eyebrow.

William Shakespeare

MEETING AT NIGHT

The grey sea and the long black land;
And the yellow half-moon large and low;
And the startled little waves that leap
In fiery ringlets from their sleep,
As I gain the cove with pushing prow,
And quench its speed i' the slushy sand.

Then a mile of warm sea-scented beach;
Three fields to cross till a farm appears;
A tap at the pane, the quick sharp scratch
And blue spurt of a lighted match,
And a voice less loud, through its joys and fears,
Than the two hearts beating each to each!

Robert Browning

SONNETT XLIII

How do I love thee? Let me count the ways.
I love thee to the depth and breadth and height
My soul can reach, when feeling out of sight
For the ends of Being and ideal Grace.
I love thee to the level of every day's
Most quiet need, by sun and candlelight.
I love thee freely, as men strive for Right;
I love thee purely, as they turn from Praise.
I love thee with the passion put to use
In my old griefs, and with my childhood's faith.
I love thee with a love I seemed to lose
With my lost saints—I love thee with the breath,
Smiles, tears, of all my life!—and, if God Choose,
I shall but love thee better after death.

Elizabeth Barrett Browning

WHEN I WAS ONE-AND-TWENTY

When I was one-and-twenty
    I heard a wise man say,
"Give crowns and pounds and guineas
    But not your heart away;
Give pearls away and rubies
    But keep your fancy free."
But I was one-and-twenty,
    No use to talk to me.

When I was one-and-twenty
    I heard him say again,
"The heart out of the bosom
    Was never given in vain;
'Tis paid with sighs a plenty
    And sold for endless rue."
And I am two-and-twenty,
    And oh, 'tis true, 'tis true.

A. E. Housman

THE KISS

I hoped that he would love me,
    And he has kissed my mouth,
But I am like a stricken bird
    That cannot reach the south

For though I know he loves me,
    Tonight my heart is sad;
His kiss was not so wonderful
    As all the dreams I had.

Sara Teasdale

ACCESSORIES

I need a seat belt for my emotions
To keep them from spilling all over the place
When I meet, head-on, the impact of your eyes.
I need a crash helmet to contain my thoughts
    explosive,
A governor to curb my racing heart,
An extra gear for these sudden shifts in feeling
From high to low and everywhere in between,
And, as a last resort,
Power brakes to put a certain S-T-O-P
To this whole high-powered affair.

Margaret Hillert

GONE

Everybody loved Chick Lorimer in our town
      Far off.
  Everybody loved her.
So we all love a wild girl keeping a hold
   On a dream she wants.
Nobody knows where Chick Lorimer went.
Nobody knows why she packed her trunk . . . a
 few old things
And is gone,
    Gone with her little chin
    Thrust ahead of her
    And her soft hair blowing careless
    From under a wide hat,
Dancer, singer, a laughing passionate lover.

Were there ten men or a hundred hunting Chick?
Were there five men or fifty with aching hearts?
   Everybody loved Chick Lorimer.
   Nobody knows where she's gone.

Carl Sandburg

LOVE'S SECRET

Never seek to tell thy love,
    Love that never told can be;
For the gentle wind does move
    Silently, invisibly.

I told my love, I told my love,
    I told her all my heart;
Trembling, cold in ghastly fears.
Ah! She did depart!

Soon as she was gone from me,
    A traveler came by,
Silently, invisibly:
He took her with a sigh.

William Blake

CASTING

Were you Paris to my Helen?
Browning to my Barrett?
Or even Damon to my Pythias?

For I know we have met—
On a different stage and different set—
Yet the feelings have always been the same.

This play I'm to stand in the wings
Waiting patiently until the end—
Until we are cast together again, friend.

Frances Hoffman

FOUR

WAR

"Even in the cannon's mouth . . ."

Then, a soldier,
Full of strange oaths, and bearded like the pard,
Jealous in honour, sudden and quick in quarrel,
Seeking the bubble reputation
Even in the cannon's mouth.

William Shakespeare

THE BATTLE

Helmet and rifle, pack and overcoat
Marched through a forest. Somewhere up ahead
Guns thudded. Like the circle of a throat
The night on every side was turning red.

They halted and they dug. They sank like moles
Into the clammy earth between the trees.
And soon the sentries, standing in their holes,
Felt the first snow. Their feet began to freeze.

At dawn the first shell landed with a crack.
Then shells and bullets swept the icy woods.
This lasted many days. The snow was black.
The corpses stiffened in their scarlet hoods.

Most clearly of that battle I remember
The tiredness in eyes, how hands looked thin
Around a cigarette, and the bright ember
Would pulse with all the life there was within.

Louis Simpson

COME UP FROM THE FIELDS FATHER

Come up from the fields father, here's a letter from our
 Pete,
And come to the front door mother, here's a letter
 from thy dear son.

Lo, 'tis autumn,
Lo, where the trees deeper green, yellower and
 redder,
Cool and sweeten Ohio's villages with leaves
 fluttering in the moderate wind,
Where apples ripe in the orchards hang and grapes on
 the trellis'd vines,
(Smell you the smell of the grapes on the vines?
Smell you the buckwheat where the bees were lately
 buzzing?)
Above all, lo, the sky so calm, so transparent after the
 rain, and with wondrous clouds,
Below too, all calm, all vital and beautiful, and the
 farm prospers well.

Down in the fields all prospers well,
But now from the fields come father, come at the
 daughter's call,
And come to the entry mother, to the front door come
 right away.

Fast as she can she hurries, something ominous, her
    steps trembling,
She does not tarry to smooth her hair nor adjust her
    cap.

Open the envelope quickly,
O this is not our son's writing, yet his name is sign'd
O a strange hand writes for our dear son, O stricken
    mother's soul!
All swims before her eyes, flashes with black, she
    catches the main words only,
Sentences broken, *gunshot wound in the breast,
    cavalry skirmish, taken to hospital,*
At present low, but will soon be better.

Ah now the single figure to me,
Amid all teeming and wealthy Ohio with all its cities
    and farms,
Sickly white in the face and dull in the head, very
    faint,
By the jamb of a door leans.

Grieve not so, dear mother (the just-grown daughter
    speaks through her sobs,
The little sisters huddle around speechless and
    dismay'd),
*See, dearest mother, the letter says Pete will soon be
    better.*

Alas poor boy, he will never be better, (nor may-be
     needs to be better that brave and simple soul),
While they stand at home at the door he is dead
     already,
The only son is dead.

But the mother needs to be better,
She with thin form presently drest in black,
By days her meals untouch'd, then at night fitfully
     sleeping, often waking,
In the midnight waking, weeping, longing with one
     deep longing,
O that she might withdraw unnoticed, silent from life
     escape and withdraw,
To follow, to seek, to be with her dear dead son.

Walt Whitman

VIETNAM

he was just back
from the war

said man they got
whites

over there now
fighting
us

and blacks over there
too

fighting us

and we can't tell
our whites
from the others

nor our blacks
from the others

& everybody
is just killing

& killing
like crazy

Clarence Major

FIVE

ADULTHOOD

"Full of wise saws . . ."

And then the justice,
In fair round belly with good capon lin'd,
With eyes severe and beard of formal cut,
Full of wise saws, and modern instances;
And so he plays his part.

William Shakespeare

CIRCLES

The white man drew a small circle in the sand
and told the red man, "This is what the Indian
knows," and drawing a big circle around the
small one, "This is what the white man knows."
The Indian took the stick and swept an immense
ring around both circles: "This is where the
white man and the red man know nothing."

Carl Sandburg

"THE BIRCH TREE"

Where is all that noise from, Mommy?
From the lot across the street, honey.
What are they doing, Mommy?
They are tearing down a birch tree, honey.
Why are they doing that, Mommy?
To make a road, honey.
What will the road do, Mommy?
It will connect cities, honey.
Will that pollute air, Mommy?
Yes it will, honey.
What will happen then, Mommy?
You ask too many questions, honey.
Go to sleep.

Peggy Savage

BOY ON A BUS

was reading
Snow White and the Seven Dwarfs

when
suddenly
a man in a nearby seat
said:

"Snow White?
Snow White is a girl's book."

And the boy
replied
without looking up from
the pages:

"But all the dwarfs are men!"

And
he
continued
reading.

Lee Bennett Hopkins

MOTHER TO SON

Well, son, I'll tell you:
Life for me ain't been no crystal stair.
It's had tacks in it,
And splinters,
And boards torn up,
And places with no carpet on the floor—
Bare.
But all the time
I'se been a-climbin' on,
And reachin' landin's,
And turnin' corners,
And sometimes goin' in the dark
Where there ain't been no light.
So, boy, don't you turn back.
Don't you set down on the steps
'Cause you find it kinder hard.
Don't you fall now—
For I'se still goin', honey,
I'se still climbin'
And life for me ain't been no crystal stair.

Langston Hughes

SIX

AGED

"... a world too wide ..."

The sixth age shifts
Into the lean and slipper'd pantaloon,
With spectacles on nose and pouch on side;
His youthful hose, well sav'd, a world too wide
For his shrunk shank; and his big manly voice,
Turning again toward childish treble, pipes
And whistles in his sound.

William Shakespeare

CHANSONS INNOCENTES I

in Just-
spring   when the world is mud-
luscious the little
lame balloonman

whistles   far   and wee

and eddieandbill come
running from marbles and
piracies and it's
spring

when the world is puddle-wonderful

the queer
old balloonman whistles
far   and   wee
and bettyandisbel come dancing

from hop-scotch and jump-rope and

it's
spring
and
    the

            goat-footed

balloonMan   whistles
far
and
wee

e. e. cummings

NO ONE WOULD BELIEVE

No one would believe
unless they saw too
as the train passed him
                    (but it's true)

facing the river
alone in the wind
an old old man
playing violin.

Charlotte Zolotow

YASE: SEPTEMBER

Old Mrs. Kawabata
cuts down the tall spike weeds—
         more in two hours
that I can get done in a day.
out of a mountain
of grass and thistle
she saved five dusty stalks
         of ragged wild blue flower
and put them in my kitchen
         in a jar.

Gary Snyder

THE BEAN EATERS

They eat beans mostly, this old yellow pair.
Dinner is a casual affair.
Plain chipware on a plain and creaking wood,
Tin flatware.

Two who are Mostly Good.
Two who have lived their day,
But keep on putting on their clothes
And putting things away.

And remembering . . .
Remembering, with twinkling and twinges,
As they lean over the beans in their rented back room
     that is full of beads and receipts and dolls
      and cloths, tobacco crumbs, vases and fringes.

Gwendolyn Brooks

EIGHTY-EIGHT

The woman

      all alone

in
apartment 16C
said,

      "Merry Christmas,"

to herself,

as she

      placed

         a plastic holly wreath

atop
a kitchen shelf.

Lee Bennett Hopkins

A SAD SONG ABOUT GREENWICH VILLAGE

She lives in a garret
　　Up a haunted stair,
And even when she's frightened
　　There's nobody to care.

She cooks so small a dinner
　　She dines on the smell,
And even if she's hungry
　　There's nobody to tell.

She sweeps her musty lodging
　　As the dawn steals near,
And even when she's crying
　　There's nobody to hear.

I haven't seen my neighbor
　　Since a long time ago,
And even if she's dead
　　There's nobody to know.

Frances Park

SEVEN

DEATH

"Last scene of all . . ."

Last scene of all,
That ends this strange eventful history,
Is second childishness and mere oblivion;
Sans teeth, sans eyes, sans taste, sans everything.

William Shakespeare

THE SECRET SITS

We dance round in a ring and suppose,
But the Secret sits in the middle and knows.

Robert Frost

GO DOWN DEATH
A FUNERAL SERMON

Weep not, weep not
She is not dead;
She's resting in the bosom of Jesus.
Heart-broken husband—weep no more;
Grief-stricken son—weep no more;
She's only just gone home.

Day before yesterday morning,
God was looking down from his great, high heaven,
Looking down on all his children,
And his eye fell on Sister Caroline,
Tossing on her bed of pain.
And God's big heart was touched with pity,
With the everlasting pity.

And God sat back on his throne,
And he commanded that tall, bright angel standing at
   his right hand:
Call me Death!
And that tall, bright angel cried in a voice
That broke like a clap of thunder:
Call Death!—Call Death!
And the echo sounded down the streets of heaven
Till it reached away back to that shadowy place,
Where Death waits with his pale, white horses.

And Death heard the summons,
And he leaped on his fastest horse,

Pale as a sheet in the moonlight.
Up the golden street Death galloped,
And the hoof of his horse struck fire from the gold,
But they didn't make no sound.
Up Death rode to the Great White Throne,
And waited for God's command.

And God said: Go down, Death, go down,
Go down to Savannah, Georgia,
Down in Yamacraw,
And find Sister Caroline.
She's borne the burden and heat of the day,
She's labored long in my vineyard,
And she's tired—
She's weary—
Go down, Death, and bring her to me.

And Death didn't say a word,
But he loosed the reins on his pale, white horse,
And he clamped the spurs to his bloodless sides,
And out and down he rode,
Through heaven's pearly gates,
Past suns and moons and stars;
On Death rode,
And the foam from his horse was like a comet in the
     sky;
On Death rode,
Leaving the lightning's flash behind;
Straight on down he came.

While we were watching round her bed,
She turned her eyes and looked away,

She saw what we couldn't see;
She saw Old Death. She saw Old Death.
Coming like a falling star.
But Death didn't frighten Sister Caroline;
He looked to her like a welcome friend,
And she whispered to us: I'm going home,
And she smiled and closed her eyes.

And Death took her up like a baby,
And she lay in his icy arms,
But she didn't feel no chill.
And Death began to ride again—
Up beyond the evening star,
Out beyond the morning star,
Into the glittering light of glory,
On to the Great White Throne.
And there he laid Sister Caroline
On the loving breast of Jesus.

And Jesus took his own hand and wiped away her
    tears,
And he smoothed the furrows from her face,
And the angels sang a little song,
And Jesus rocked her in his arms,
And kept a-saying: Take your rest,
Take your rest, take your rest.
Weep not—weep not,
She's not dead;
She's resting in the bosom of Jesus.

James Weldon Johnson

from
JULIUS CAESAR

Cowards die many times before their deaths;
The valiant never taste of death but once.
Of all the wonders that I yet have heard,
It seems to me most strange that men should fear;
Seeing that death, a necessary end,
Will come when it will come.

William Shakespeare

DEATH

Each soul
changing its mount
for the unending ride
on life's merry-go-round through Time
Unchanged.

Frances Hoffman

LIFE ROUNDED WITH SLEEP

The babe is at peace within the womb;
The corpse is at rest within the tomb:
  We begin in what we end.

Percy Bysshe Shelley

INDEX OF POETS

INDEX OF TITLES

INDEX OF FIRST LINES